Gamiani, or Two Passionate Nights

Gamiani, or Two Passionate Nights

Alfred de Musset

MINT EDITIONS

Gamiani, or Two Passionate Nights was first published in 1833.

This edition published by Mint Editions 2021.

ISBN 9781513295329 | E-ISBN 9781513295473

Published by Mint Editions®

 MINT
EDITIONS

minteditionbooks.com

Publishing Director: Jennifer Newens
Design & Production: Rachel Lopez Metzger
Project Manager: Micaela Clark
Typesetting: Westchester Publishing Services

Contents

Extract from the Memoirs
of the Countess of C*** Concerning
the Author of Gamiani

During my stay in a certain house, I had occasion to exercise my quarrelsome disposition against a man whose glory, although it may have been brilliant, scarcely sufficed to atone for his manners.

It goes without saying that I shall not say who he was; if anyone recognizes him, my conscience will be perfectly easy on that point, for it will be rather his fault than mine. I do not feel at all shy of mentioning my connection with him, for, as we shall see, the story of our amours is not an exchange of mere caresses, but a rapid succession of brutal attacks, of quarrels and ugly pleasantries.

The first time I set eyes on him was, I think, the day after we had been to the Chaumiere, and I was not at all in a good temper—the impression he made on me is almost impossible to describe. I was asked to follow Fanny into the small boudoir and did so. There was a man sitting by the fire with his back turned to me. He had very fair hair, and was thin, but of medium stature.

I went forward a little; he was beating time on his knee with his fingers: his hands were thin, his fingers white and long. I went and sat opposite him: he raised his eyes and looked me in the face. I gazed at this juvenile wreck. One should have called him a ghost rather than a man, for he could hardly have been thirty years of age, in spite of the wrinkles that furrowed his face.

"Where have you come from?" he asked as though waking from a dream. "I don't know you!"

I made no answer, he began to curse.

"Will you answer me, when I do you the honor of addressing you?" I blushed furiously and said:

"Do I ask you who you are or where you come from? Am I obliged to show you all my papers to stand before you? I tell you at once that I haven't got any."

He continued to look at me with a stupified air. I moved away towards the door.

"Stay here!" he cried, "I order it."

I did not stop to hear more, but went out.

I went to tell the fat woman what had just happened. She shrugged her shoulders and said that I had been wrong, that this gentleman was her greatest friend; she wanted him to be treated well, that he often came to spend a week in her house; furthermore that he was very interesting, in fact one of the greatest literary men of the age.

"What! That fellow?" I cried, astonished. "Yes, that fellow."

"Well then, I should advise him to write less and to speak more politely."

Denise was there. She bent down and whispered in my ear: "Oh, she's quite taken up with him because he has lots of money; but he's a rotten fellow, brutal, rude, and always the worse for drink. I am sorry for those who fall in love with him."

A furious ring at the bell resounded through the house. It was my enemy who was angry because I had left him alone.

"Don't go back," said Denise.

"On the contrary, I shall," I replied, casting an ironical glance at the fat woman. "I was rather glad to have an opportunity of coming into contact with a genius. There is always something to be gained in the society of clever people."

I returned to the boudoir.

"Ah, there you are again," he said. "In this house, everyone obeys me. So you will do the same."

"Perhaps."

"There's no perhaps about it, and to begin with, you have got to have a drink with me!"

He rang the bell. Fanny quickly appeared.

"Bring something to drink!" he ordered.

She came back with three bottles and two glasses.

"Well, what would you like? Will you take a drop of rum, brandy or absinthe?"

"Thanks very much, but I only drink wine with water in it, and I am not at all thirsty just now."

"What the devil has that got to do with me? You've got to drink with me!" "No!" I answered, most decidedly.

He swore like a trooper, and having filled up a glass with absinthe, tossed it off at a gulp.

"Now its your turn. Drink, or I'll beat you."

He filled up both glasses, and brought one to me, with tottering steps. I watched him, rather frightened by his threat, as he came towards me, but I was determined not to give way.

I calmly took the glass he offered me, and threw the contents into the fire.

"Oh," he cried, as he took hold of my hand and twisted me round, but without hurting me, "you are disobedient. Well, well, so much the better, I prefer that!"

He took a handful of gold from his pocket in one hand, and a glass of liquor in the other:

"Drink," he cried, "and I will give you all this." "I will not drink it." I answered.

"Oh" he said, laughing and bowing a little, "what a splendid character! Touched neither by fear nor cupidity! That doesn't matter, I like you as you are."

"Come and sit by me on the sofa and tell me your story." I sat down without a word.

"You have been unhappy and persecuted, have you not? I will wager that like your companions here, your father was at least a general. Be perfectly frank about it, do you like me?"

"I dislike you very much."

"All right. You are not like other girls. They are all crazy about me. But what will you? One cannot control one's sympathies. I can't bear the others, but as to you, you seem to be out of the ordinary, and I like you. Take this gold. You have done nothing to earn it! I make you a present of it. Take it and go away. Leave me!"

I made haste to take him at his word. I turned as I was going out, just in time to see him pouring himself out a glass of brandy.

Denise was waiting for me at the door.

"I was afraid he might hurt you," she said; "it seems that when anyone makes him cross, he strikes them, so I was listening in case I should have to come to your assistance."

I thanked her, smiling. At that time, I was holding my life very cheaply, and if he had struck me for the pleasure of torturing me, of humiliating me, I think he would have run greater danger than I. I had snubbed him so terribly that he seemed lost without me. He used to come to see me three or four times a day. He had his mad moments in which he said the most frightful things without rhyme or reason.—That exasperated me, and I declared I would no longer go down when he called. But I was soon given to understand that I was no longer my own mistress. I began to positively hate the fat woman, I went down in a perfect fury, and without giving him the time to say a word, I began:

"What do you want with me? What do you want to insist on seeing me for? The very sight of you disgusts me. If it's in your drunken nights that you write the beautiful things which I read this morning, I am really sorry for you, for the next morning you surely are not able to recognize the author, and that's a pity! It doesn't become you to slight women and run them down! You are less than a libertine, you are only a drunkard! If one woman has served you badly, that's no excuse for hating the others."

"Perhaps you are right to disdain us, but in that case, let us alone!" I was rather worried as to how he would take this speech the beginning of which made him open his haggard eyes. But I soon had reason for calming my nerves, for he had dropped off to sleep in the armchair."

I crept out on tiptoe.

It appeared that he was not offended with me, for the next day he came and asked leave to take me out to dine with him. Madame quickly said he might do so, without consulting me. I comforted myself with the thought that he kept his vulgar eccentricities for inside the house, and that in other places he would show more self- respect.

So the shameless libertine would give way to the man of taste, to the eminent writer. He came at six o'clock and took me to the celebrated restaurant the "Rocher de Cancale." I was simply dressed in a new hat and frock. I was pleased with my appearance; I did not feel quite so sad, because for the second time I had got away from that dreadful house. At first, there was not so much to complain of in his behaviour, except a few jokes of rather poor taste, which I reproved as well as I could.

The waiter brought us a bottle of soda water.

I could never have conceived the mad idea that had suddenly possessed this extraordinary man who had chosen me as the victim of his caprice. He took the bottle of soda water to open it as if he was going to drink some, turned it towards me, and drenched me with it from head to foot.

There may be times in one's life and moments of good temper when one might have taken it for a joke. But I was so miserable that this seeming fit of madness set me in a rage.

I burst into a torrent of tears; my tears were the tears of anger. But the more I sobbed, the more he laughed.

　　　　　　　　　　　　ALFRED DE MUSSET

First Part

Midnight was striking, and Countess Gamiani's reception rooms were still sparkling with a thousand lights.

The dancers were warming up to the sounds of a bewitching band in round dances and quadrilles. The ladies dresses were marvellous, the jewels a brilliant sight.

The fête had been organized at a vast expense, and the mistress of the house, gracious and smiling for all her guests, seemed happy at her success. One after another came to her to murmur their thanks in complimentary terms and this only added to her contentment.

As usual, I was satisfied to be a mere looker-on, but I had already remarked more than one detail that disinclined me to ascribe to Countess Gamiani all the virtues with which she was usually credited. I had already judged her as a woman of society. The task remained for me to dissect her moral character, to lay bare the region of her heart: and I do not know what strange, uneasy, incomprehensible feeling held me back in this probing of her nature. I felt I should have infinite trouble in penetrating this woman's existence, perhaps because her conduct threw no light on it.

Still in the flower of her youth, with a considerable fortune, pretty enough for most people, this woman without relatives, without close friends, had to a certain extent carved out an individual position for herself. She was apparently spending on herself means that could easily have borne sharing with a partner in life.

Many little scandals had been whispered concerning her, but for lack of proof of any of the rumours, she always remained a mystery.

Some said she was like Balzac's Feodora, a woman having neither heart nor passions: others imagined she had had some cruel disappointment in life, that had left her desirous of shunning any other liaison for fear of betrayal.

I wanted to know the truth; I used every artifice my mind could devise, but all in vain; I could never come to any satisfactory solution of the mystery.

Feeling piqued at my continued failure, I was going away from the scene, when an old roué standing behind me, said loud enough for me to hear: "Pooh, she's a tribade, a Lesbian."

This was like a flash of lightning to me: I immediately thought of a thousand reasons for believing this, there could be no mistake.

A tribade! Ah! this word sounds strangely in ones ears. Then it raises in ones mind I know not what murky images of unheard of sensations, lustful in the extreme. It means voluptuous madness, unbridled vice, a criminal enjoyment that is ever incomplete.

Vainly I strove to thrust these ideas from me; for a time my imagination ran riot. I closed my eyes, only to see the Countess before me, nude, in another woman's arms, her hair undone and streaming around her panting body, always tormented with half-satisfied desire.

My veins seemed filled with liquid fire, my senses reeled, I fell back half unconscious on a sofa.

As I came to myself, I coolly thought out a plan for taking the Countess unawares: I felt I must do that at all costs.

I made up my mind to watch her that night, to conceal myself somewhere in her bedroom. The glass door of her dressing room faced the bed. I knew that. I realised at once the advantage of that spot; and hiding between dresses hung up, so that I could see unseen, I resolved to patiently await the orgy.

I was scarcely safely hidden there, when I saw the Countess enter her bedroom.

She called her maid, a dark-complexioned young girl with a striking figure, and said: "Julia, I shan't want you this evening, go to bed. . . Ah, if you hear any noise in my room, don't take any notice, I want to be alone."

These words seemed to promise me something dramatic. I congratulated myself on my boldness in hiding there.

Gradually the guests' voices from the drawing room faded away: the Countess was alone with one of her friends, Mademoiselle Fanny B. . . They were soon both together in the bedroom before my eyes.

FANNY: What a nuisance! Its raining in torrents, and not a carriage left.

GAMIANI: I am just as sorry as you are; unfortunately my carriage is being repaired at the coach-builders.

FANNY: My mother will be worrying.

GAMIANI: Never fear, my dear Fanny. I have sent to let your mother know that you are spending the night with me. I can very well put you up.

FANNY: You are really too kind. I'm afraid I shall be troubling you.

GAMIANI: Say rather, you will be giving me great pleasure. It is an adventure that I shall enjoy. . . I am not going to send you off to sleep in another room, you can stay with me here.

FANNY: Why? I should only keep you from sleeping.

GAMIANI: Oh, you must not stand on ceremony. . . Come, my dear, let us be like two school-girl friends together.

(A sweet kiss here interrupted these affectionate words.)

I will help you to undress. My maid has gone to bed, but we can do without her. How beautiful she is made! Happy child to have such a figure.

FANNY: Do you really think its nice?

GAMIANI: Charming!

FANNY: You want to make me vain!

GAMIANI: Oh, marvellous, how snowy white! I am quite jealous!

FANNY: As far as that goes, I don't agree with you, your skin is whiter than mine.

GAMIANI: Not at all, child! But take everything off, the same as I do. Oh what a fuss you make; one would think you were undressing in front of a man. There, look in the glass. Paris himself would award you the apple. . . Little rascal, she's laughing to see herself so lovely. You deserve a kiss on the forehead, on the cheeks, and on the lips. . . She is sweetly pretty everywhere, all over.

The Countess' lips and mouth lingered busily at all points of Fanny's body. Fanny was timid, astonished, trembling, but she lay still and let her do what she would, not understanding.

They formed a lovely couple in their sensuality, their grace, their lascivious abandonment, and the shy modesty of the young girl. She looked like a virgin, an angel in the arms of a raging bacchante.

What beauties were displayed to my sight, what a spectacle to excite all my desires I

FANNY: Oh what are you doing? Oh, please, please let me go, madame.

GAMIANI: No, no, Fanny my sweet, my child, my life, my joy I You are too lovely, do you know! I love you, I adore you! I am mad for you!

Vainly the young girl struggled to get away, her cries were smothered in kisses. Pressed, held in a grip, all resistance was useless: the Countess, in her wild embrace, carried her bodily over to her bed and threw her down as though she was a wild beast carrying her prey to her lair.

FANNY: What is the matter with you? Oh, my God, Madam I but that is terrible! I shall scream, leave me alone! . . . you frighten me!

But to all her desperate cries the only response was kisses, more intense and rapid than before. Both the women grappled till their enlacing arms made of two bodies only one, it seemed.

GAMIANI: Fanny, give yourself to me, be all, all mine! There, I give you all my life! There, that is true pleasure! . . . how you are trembling, my dear child! Ah, you are giving way at last!
FANNY: But that is very wrong, you shouldn't do it, you are killing me. . . oh, I am surely dying!
GAMIANI: Yes, hold me tighter, don't let me go, my sweet, my loved one I How lovely she is in the delight of her lust I You are coming, you are happy! Oh, God!

It was then really an extraordinary sight to watch.

The Countess with her eyes bloodshot and staring, her hair flying from her head, rushed with twisting body on her victim, who was in turn very moved and excited by the novelty of her sensations. They both gripped each other as if they never could let go. They both bounded up and down; their mutual attacks stifled their cries, their sighs were dissolved in kisses.

The impetuous assaults of the Countess made the bed creak and shake. Fanny was, however, soon vanquished, and let her arms fall exhausted to her side. She was deathly pale, and lay like a lifeless statue of ivory.

The Countess was raving mad. The pleasure had bereft her of her reason, but had not satisfied her. She leapt like a crazy thing into the middle of the room, rolled on the carpet, exciting herself by her own lascivious poses, thrusting her fingers into the seat of her pleasure.

When I saw this I lost my head.

For a moment I had been overwhelmed by disgust and indignation: I thought of appearing before the Countess, and crushing her with scornful words. But my sensual feelings mastered my reason. The flesh triumphed over the mind, thrilled me in every fibre. I was bewildered, crazy. I rushed forward and threw myself on the beautiful nude Fanny, my veins standing out on my forehead, my whole nature on fire.

She had hardly had time to grasp that she was being attacked in some other way, before I felt her supple young body tremble and then heave under me, advancing to meet me, and giving me stroke for stroke.

Our tongues began to meet and cross each other the most passionate kisses. Our very souls seemed to melt into one.

FANNY: Oh! My God, I am being killed. . .

As she gasped these words, the beautiful body stiffened and fell back as she drenched me with her liquid favours.

"Ah, Fanny," I cried "wait a moment, now its your turn. . . to receive the shower. . . ah!

I thought all my life was leaving my veins. What an excess of pleasure! Completely exhausted, buried in Fanny's embraces, I had felt nothing of the Countess' terrible attacks.

Brought to herself by our cries, by our smothered love-words, transported by desire and jealousy, she had thrown herself upon me to tear me away from her little girl- sweetheart.

She shook me, clasped me in her arms, dug her nails into my flesh, bit me wherever she could.

This double contact of the two bodies streaming with pleasure, burning with desire, awakened my amorous feelings still more, goaded them to the highest pitch.

I was being burned up by passion on every side. I stayed firm and victorious, in Fanny's possession: and then, without yielding my position at all, lay in this strange medley of three bodies, I succeeded in firmly seizing the Countess' thighs, and holding them widely opened over my head.

"Gamiani," I cried, a come to me, a little farther forward, supporting your weight on your arms."

Gamiani understood what I wanted, and I was able to fully enjoy running my agile and devouring tongue up and down her fiery slit.

Fanny, quite beside herself, lost to her surroundings, lovingly caressed the palpitating breast that moved up and down above her head.

A moment later, the Countess was finished off, avowed herself conquered.

GAMIANI: What fires have you lighted in me? It is too much. . . Have pity. . . Oh, what a terrible, lustful sport! You are killing me. . . God! . . . I am choking.

Her body fell heavily on one side like a dead thing. Fanny, still more excited than at first, threw her arms round my neck, pressed me to her, embraced me fondly and then crossed her legs over my loins.

FANNY: Oh, my dear fellow, come to me again, give it to me all. . . don't go too quickly, . . . there, stop. . . now go on again. . . there, ah! . . . quicker. . . go on. . . oh, now I can feel it all through me. . . I'm coming. . . swimming in it. . . I. . .

Here she lay exhausted and I was almost lifelessly stretched out on her beautiful form. Our lips had melted into an unspeakably long, liquid kiss to which there could be no end. We were speechless, breathless.

At last we recovered consciousness, we rose all three of us, and cast bewildered glances around.

As if ashamed of her abandonment, the Countess hastily threw a dressing gown round her superb figure. Fanny hid herself under the bedclothes and we looked at each other for a moment without a word.

Suddenly Fanny, like a child caught out in some forbidden foolishness burst into tears; the Countess began to scold me.

GAMIANI: "Sir, you ought to be heartily ashamed of yourself for taking two innocent women by surprise. . . It is a disgraceful trap you have set for us. . . you make me blush for myself!"

I attempted to defend myself, but she went on:

"Oh sir, you must know that a woman never pardons a man who discovers her weaknesses." I retorted as well as I could that she had inspired a most unhappy passion in my breast, that her coldness had maddened me, and that I could not help it.

"Besides," I added, "can you think for a moment, Gamiani, that I would ever take advantage of a secret that I have discovered more by chance than by design. As long as I live I cannot forget the great pleasures we have known together, but shall always keep the secret to myself. If you think I am to blame, you have only to think that I was frantic with the sight before me, and that I shall only keep the memory of the pleasure that we have enjoyed, and can enjoy again together."

Turning to Fanny, while the Countess turned her head away, and pretended to be very ashamed. . .

"Mademoiselle, shed no tears for the pleasure you have experienced. Oh! think only of the sweet and happy moments we have just spent together; let them remain in your memory as a happy dream, which belongs to you alone, which no one else will ever know of. I swear to you, I will never spoil the sweet thought of my happiness by revealing it to a third person."

Her anger seemed to calm down, her tears to cease to flow, and we soon found ourselves, without knowing why, all three reunited in the caresses and the kisses of love.

"Oh, my lovely girls, let not any fear or anxiety trouble you more! Let us give ourselves up unreservedly to pleasure, to sensuality. . . as if this were the last night we have to spend on earth!"

GAMIANI: The die is cast: let us give ourselves up to enjoyment; Come on, Fanny! . . . kiss me, come you crazy thing. . . I want to bite you, to suck your tenderest parts, to imbibe you, to draw you out to the marrow of your bones. Alcide mount her, cover her. . . oh, what a splendid thing you've got. . . what a fortune that is!

ALCIDE: You are envious of that pleasure, Gamiani, why don't you take it yourself then?

You scorn this form of pleasure, you will be delighted with it when you have tasted it. Don't get up. . . Bring forward that part of you that I must now attack. Ah; what beauties you display, what a position! Come, Fanny, quick squat down on top of the Countess, and guide my dart, my fiery dart, into her inmost sanctuary. Go ahead, no. . . that's too quick, too vigorous. Ah, Gamiani, you are trying to get the pleasure too quickly.

The Countess was wriggling like a little devil, paying more attention to Fanny's kisses than to my efforts to satisfy her. Then I took advantage of a movement that upset the equilibrium to throw Fanny over on top of the Countess and to assault her furiously. In an instant we were all three mingled, showering down in one stream of love. . .

GAMIANI: What a caprice of yours, Alcide, you have suddenly gone over to the enemy. . . Oh! I freely forgive you, for you have realised that it is useless to waste time on a woman who cannot appreciate. But what can I say? I feel only too sadly that I have divorced from nature. I am all the time dreaming, imagining, feeling excitement from the horrible alone. Nothing that is not extravagant, unnatural, can appeal to me now; I am ever seeking the unattainable. Oh, I assure you it is dreadful to feel as I do! To spoil one's inmost feelings, to be consumed with a desire that is not to be appeased. My diseased imagination is slowly killing me. I am frightfully unhappy.

As she spoke, her every gesture, every changing shade of her facial expression displayed only too well the truth of what she said. It was really pitiable to witness the manner in which this unhappy woman was suffering from her fatal passions.

"This is perhaps only a passing phase with you, dear Gamiani," said I, "you give your mind up too much to bad books."

GAMIANI: Oh, no, no! it is not I. . .
      Listen, you will perhaps pity me, or at least excuse me, if I tell you my true story. . .

I was brought up in Italy by my aunt who was left a widow when still quite young. When I had reached my fifteenth year, I was awfully ignorant and knew nothing of the world around me except the terrors of our religion.

Entirely devoted to God, I spent my time praying Heaven to spare me the tortures of Hell.

My aunt encouraged these fears without ever soothing them by the least show of kindness towards me. . .

The only peaceful moments I found were those of the night, when I could sleep. My days were as miserable as those of one condemned to death.

Only rarely did my aunt allow me to visit her in the early morning in her bedroom. Then she took me into bed with her. She drew me to her bosom, she made me lie between her thighs, and suddenly, I remember, used to press me convulsively to her, to throw her limbs around me, her head back, and would laugh hysterically all the while.

I was terribly afraid of her at these times and thought she was subject to fits. . .

At last one day, after she had been talking a long time with a Franciscan friar, she called me to her, and the reverend father began to address me as follows:

"My child, you are getting a big girl now. The devil, who is always seeking to tempt us, can see you always. Very soon you may begin to feel his attacks. Only if you are pure and immaculate, his darts cannot reach you; if you are without reproach you will remain invulnerable.

By pain and suffering, Our Lord has redeemed the world, by his martyrdom and by your own punishments, you may expiate your own sins.

You must prepare to undergo the martyrdom of the redemption. Ask God to give you the strength and bravery needful: this night you will be put to the test. . . Go in peace, my daughter."

My aunt had already spoken to me a short time before, of the punishment, of the torture one must suffer in order to obtain pardon for ones sins. When the monk left us, I was quite frightened about what he had said. . . As I found myself alone. I wanted to pray, to think of God alone, but nothing came before my mind except the thought of the penance that I had to undergo.

My aunt woke me up in the middle of the night. She ordered me to strip naked, she washed me from head to foot, and dressed me in a long black gown tight at the neck, but entirely divided all the way down the back.

She was dressed in exactly the same curious fashion, and we left the house together in a carriage.

An hour later, I was with her in a vast hall, hung with black drapery, and lit only by one lamp hanging from the ceiling.

In the middle there was a praying-stool surrounded by cushions. "Kneel down, my dear niece: prepare yourself with prayer to bear with patience and bravery all the punishment that God sees fit to inflict upon you."

I had scarcely had the time to obey her orders, when a secret door was opened: a monk, dressed in black like us approached me, mumbled a few words, and then pulling my frock open and letting the sides down, exposed all the hinder portion of my body.

He sighed and seemed to shudder, and his hand, doubtless 'because the sight of my white skin excited him, began to wander all over my back, lingered a moment on my bottom, and finished by pressing in lower down.

"It is by this part that woman sins," he uttered in a sepulchral voice "it is by these lower parts that she must suffer!"

He had scarcely pronounced these words, when I felt the terrible strokes of rods, of knotted cords rendered still more terrible by bits of steel wire inserted in their strands.

I clasped the back of the praying stool, I tried my best to stifle my cries, but it was in vain: the pain was too frightful. I rushed out into the hall, crying "Pity, have pity on me! I cannot bear such torture, kill me if you will, but let me be!"

"Miserable little coward," cried my aunt, "you should see what I bear." As she said this, she showed herself courageously quite naked, spread her thighs wide open, and held her bottom lifted up high.

The blows fell pitilessly upon her, and in a moment, her thighs were streaming in blood.

My aunt seemed to be unmoved. From time to time she cried: "Go on, harder! Oh! still harder!"

The sight of this took me out of myself, I felt a superhuman courage, and I shouted that I was ready to bear anything.

My aunt immediately got up, and covered me with hot kisses, meanwhile the monk, tied my hands behind me, and blindfolded my eyes.

What shall I tell you? Only that the torture began to be more unbearable than before: and very soon, quite stupefied by the pain, I lay motionless, I could no longer feel anything.

Only I remember, that through the sound of the blows, I could hear confusedly, as if afar off, the sound of kisses, little cries, of hands smacking on naked limbs. There were also nervous, crazy, maddening little laughs, which I knew later to be the forerunners of amorous joys. Sometimes I recognized my aunt's voice, as she groaned with pleasure, sounding above this unreal harmony, this bloody festival.

It was only later on that I began to understand that this spectacle of my punishment had served to awaken their unholy desires, each one of my stifled groans had stimulated them to amorous extravagances.

At last, probably tired, my executioner stopped thrashing me. Still like one lifeless, I was half dead from fright, I was quite resigned to die. However, I must confess, as I gradually recovered consciousness, I began to feel a most unusual excitement: my whole body was trembling, fire seemed to be running through me.

I began to squirm and writhe about, as if filled with unknown desire, and then, all at once two brawny arms seized me; and something, I knew not what, something long and stiff and warm, came and stood between my thighs, glided lower down and finally was thrust into my deepest parts. Just then, I thought I was being split in two. I gave a frightful cry, but only mocking laughter answered me. Two or three formidable pushes sufficed to lodge this terrible weapon right inside me. My thighs all smothered with blood, seemed to adhere to the thighs of my enemy; it felt as though our two bodies were melting into one. My temples were throbbing, my nerves overstrung to breaking point. The vigorous pushing, and its rapidity, burnt my inside so terribly that I thought red-hot iron was thrust into my vitals.

Soon however, I felt ecstatic, I was beside myself, but fancied I must have ascended to heaven. A creamy, sticky, boiling liquid then ran into me, searched my bones, penetrated to my spinal marrow. . . Oh, that was too delightful, I melted too, I felt turned to molten lava. I could feel such an active, living, devouring stream pouring from me, I caused more to flow from him also by heaving madly to meet the attacker and fell at last into an abyss of endless sensual delight.

FANNY: Oh! Gamiani, what a description, you set the devil in me loose.

GAMIANI: But that was not all.

The pleasure that had overpowered me soon changed to intolerable agony, I was cruelly ravished. More than twenty monks threw themselves upon my wounded body like hungry cannibals one after the other. My head fell helplessly to one side. My ruined, broken poor little body lay a wreck on the pillows, I lay like a corpse till they carried me away and laid me in my bed.

FANNY: What infamous cruelty!

GAMIANI: Oh, yes, it was infamous and still more horrible than that.

I was ill from it, but when I came to myself and was gradually won back to health and strength, I realized the shocking perversity of my aunt and her debauched companions, who were so sunken in vice that nothing stimulated their beastly desires except the sight of fearful torture. I vowed a mortal hatred on them all, and in my heart, filled with a crying lust of vengeance, I held forever an undying hatred of men.

The mere idea of submitting to their touch has always repelled me. I have never consented to serve as a vile toy for any man's lust.

A fiery temperament had been awakened within me, and I had to cool it in some way or other. Nothing cured me of masturbating myself but the clever lessons of the nuns of the Redemptorist Convent.—Their fatal teachings have damned me forever.

Here the Countess broke down, sobbing. Kisses and caresses failed to comfort this poor woman.

To change the subject, I turned to Fanny.

ALCIDE: Now its your turn, you beautiful wondering girl! Now there you are initiated in a single night into many mysteries. Come along now, be a good girl and tell us what you think of it, what feelings the revelation of sensuality has awakened in you.

FANNY: Oh, I must confess, I dare not tell you, I feel shy!

ALCIDE: But your modesty is now a little out of season.

FANNY: No, but after all the Countess has related, what little I could say would not be worth listening to.

ALCIDE: Nonsense, my poor little dove! Go ahead, why feel shy? Are we not confederates in the pleasures of love? We have no longer cause to blush, either of us. We have tried everything, we can relate all we have done.

GAMIANI: Come along, my dear, I'll give you a kiss, two, a hundred if need be to get you to make up your mind. And look at Alcide. . . he is quite in love! Look, he is threatening you with his weapon.

FANNY: No, no, leave me alone. Alcide, I have not an atom of strength left. Have pity on me. . . Gamiani, how terrible you are! Alcide get off. . . Oh!

ALCIDE: I give no quarter, by Jove! Either you're going to tell us the adventures of your maidenhead, or Marcus Gurtius will ride fully armed into the breach!

FANNY: Oh, well, if you force me to, I s'pose I must. . .

GAMIANI and ALCIDE:—Yes, yes! begin. . .

FANNY: Up to my fifteenth year I was quite ignorant of everything. I swear to you its true. I had never even given a thought to any difference between the sexes.

I lived free from care, happy, I suppose, when one day it was terribly hot, and I was alone in my room at home.

I thought how nice it would be to take my things off and to lie quite free and cool, so I undressed and lay on a cool ottoman; I was practically naked. . . Even now, I feel ashamed to tell you. . . I stretched out full length, I spread my thighs wide apart, I turned and twisted in every possible posture. And without thinking what I was doing, I must have presented quite an indecent sight.

The leather covering of the ottoman was icy cold. This caused such an agreeable sensation, a sort of voluptuous smoothing of the whole of my body. Oh! how freely I could breathe, surrounded by a warm atmosphere, and the warmth seemed to penetrate me. What a soft, ravishing feeling! I seemed to float in a delightful ecstasy. I felt as though new life were flooding my being, that I had renewed my strength, I had grown taller, that I inhaled a god-like air, that I was blossoming out in the warm rays of a beneficent sunshine.

ALCIDE: You are getting poetical, Fanny.

FANNY: Oh, I am simply describing exactly what I felt.

My eyes wandered gently over my own body, I stroked my neck, I held my bosoms. And then my fingers wandered farther downwards, and pressed in, and stopped there, and in spite of myself I fell into a deep reverie.

The words "love" and "lover" rang, ceaselessly in my ears, with their mysterious sound, that I did not understand.

At last I felt lonely. I forgot that I had my parents, my friends. I felt a shocking emptiness in my heart.

I got up, and looked sadly round me.

I remained pensive for a while, hanging my head in a most melancholic way, my arms hanging down, my hands locked together.

Then as I looked myself over, as I began to touch every little secret part, I wondered if this had not all its meaning, its destined use.

Instinctively I felt that something was lacking, something that I could not define, but that I wanted, and desired with all my soul.

I must have looked insane, for from time to time I gave a little laugh of madness, and my arms were stretched out in an empty embrace as if to hold the object of my desires to my heart. I went so far as to embrace my own body. I touched myself, I stroked myself, I kissed my arms, I felt I could not live without a reality, a living body that I might hold, and caress and love: in my strange hallucination, I caressed myself, with the phantasy that I was attaching myself to another.

Through the windows, far away one could see the trees, the green meadows, and I felt tempted to go out and roll in the grass, or to climb up high in the branches. Then I looked at the sky and thought I should like to fly in the air, to mingle with the vapours, with the clouds, the blue of the ether and the angels.

I felt I should go mad: the blood rushing hotly to my head. No longer knowing what I was doing, I had thrown myself on the sofa and seizing bolsters and cushions, held one tight between my fat young thighs and another in my arms. This one I kissed and caressed, I think I even wasted smiles on it, I was so intoxicated by the tumult of my newly awakened senses.

All at once I stopped, I shuddered, I fancied that I was dissolving into liquid love. "Ah! my Goodness, ah!" I cried. And I got up terribly frightened at myself, I was quite wet through down below.

Not being able to understand in the least what had really happened, I thought I had hurt myself in some way, that I was wounded; I was in a shocking fright. I fell on my knees and prayed that God would forgive me if I had done wrong.

ALCIDE: Sweet innocent little thing! And you did not tell a soul what had frightened you so dreadfully?

FANNY: No, never! I should not have dared to do so, I was still ignorant only an hour ago of the truth; you have taught me the right answer to all my questioning.

ALCIDE: Oh, Fanny! This confession sets the seal of delight on my happiness. My dear little friend, you shall now receive a further proof of my ardour. Gamiani, excite me, so that I may drench this young flower with heavenly dew.

GAMIANI: What fire, what ardour, Fanny, you are already swooning with pleasure. . . Oh, she is coming. . . she is really coming. . .

FANNY: Oh, Alcide, Alcide, I am dying. . . I. . .

And the sweetness of the forbidden fruit consumed us with its intoxication, bore us both into celestial regions.

After a few moments of repose, having regained my coolness, my presence of mind, I began to speak as follows:

ALCIDE: I am the child of young and healthy parents. I had a happy childhood, without tears or sickness, so at the age of thirteen. I was already quite manly. The spur of sexual desire began at this early age to made itself felt.

Destined for the Church, brought up in all the rigor of chastity, I fought against the first symptoms of carnal desire with all my childish strength. My flesh began to awaken, tormented me, powerful and imperious, and I thrust it pitilessly back from me.

I resolved to fast most rigorously. At night, during my sleep, nature found its own solution, and I was horribly afraid of the visible result, as though it was my fault. I increased the strictness of my abstinence and my care to avoid all sinful thoughts. This continual internal strife finally brought me to a stupid and idiotic state of mind.

My constrained abstinence caused a sensitiveness or rather an irritation in my nervous system, that I had never suspected before.

I often felt giddy, it seemed to me that everything was turning round and I was spinning round also. If my eyes chanced to fall on a young girl, she appeared instantly to me to be some fairy princess resplendent with a thousand magic lights.

The humour of my body, too copious and ever overheated, ran to my head, and its waves beating against the walls of my brain, caused me a sort of dazzling mirage.

This morbid condition had lasted for several months, when one morning I felt all at once a violent contraction and tension in all my limbs, followed by a terrible and convulsive movement, as if I was going to have an epileptic fit. The sensation of dazzling lights before my eyes returned with renewed force. I thought I could see a black wheel turning before me, it expanded, its rim filled the universe: then from the centre a ball of light shed its rays over all the circumference.

An endless horizon seemed to stretch away around me, a phantasmagoria of rockets and showers of fire seemed to fill the heavens above my head, and then fell iit showers of emerald green, sapphire blue and heavenly azure.

The blinding light died away, a velvety deep blue night, soft and dark, but luminous took its place, like the mysterious shimmer of an unseen moon, and then from the extremest point of the boundless distance there came to me a cohort of delicious naked girls, like golden-winged butterflies, magnificent in the splendour of their alabaster nudity.

I rose to meet them, but they escaped from my too eager grasp, laughing and mocking me. For an instant they faded from my sight, then they appeared again, more active, more joyous: charming bouquets of smiling young faces who sent smiles, alluring glances in my direction.

Little by little, the dream of maidens vanished from my sight; it was succeeded by visions of riper girls, women matured to all the passions of love.

Some of them were living and palpitating Venuses; others pale and melancholy as the virgins of Ossian. Their delicate forms, voluptuous in their contours, faded from my view under clouds of vaporous atmosphere; they seemed to die away, weary of waiting for my embrace, they held out their arms, but vanished always from my eager sight.

I was a prey to the most terrible sensual urge, I rose to my feet, my spine and muscles quite rigid, and rubbed my glorious standing priapus up and down like a madman. I spoke out loud to myself of love, of pleasure; in the most frantically indecent terms, I seemed to see Jupiter in his clouds of fire; Juno directing the thunderbolts; I saw all Olympus in the disorder of a genesic fever, an extraordinary mêlée; after that, I was witness to an orgy, a hellish bacchanal feast.

Hundreds of satyrs, with their cloven hoofs and horned heads, ran round in an infernal cave lighted by blue and red torches, and the grotesqueness of their gestures made an indescribably lascivious scene. Some of them there were, on swings, rushing through the air with their far outstanding weapons brandishing their menace, entered the women in their way, penetrating their bodies with their darts, causing them an unutterable pain, as rapid as unexpected. Others, full of mischief, turned a prudish matron over, head downwards, and with insane laughter brought a ram, whose great fiery priapus they directed into her body, driving her crazy with lecherous manœuvres. Still others could be seen with the burning slow-match firing cannon, from which issued monstrous members that were buried with lightning swiftness between the wide-spread thighs of a frenzied she-devil.

The most spiteful of the lot bound a Messalina down by her four limbs and indulged in her sight in the most frightful sexual excesses. The unhappy woman foamed at the mouth, twisted about, raved for a pleasure that was denied her.

Here and there, in every imaginable corner, there were a thousand little sprites, little demons, every one uglier, more lively or more sneaking than the other, who came and went from one to the other, sucking, pinching, biting, dancing in rings, mixing together. Everywhere it was only laughter, screams, convulsions, fits of madness, cries, sighs, faintings from excessively voluptuous feelings.

On a raised platform, the devils of the highest rank were amusing themselves by producing a parody of our religion, and its mysteries.

A nun perfectly naked, kneeling at all her length, her eyes turned up in the most heavenly manner to the top of the nave, was receiving in the most devotional way the white communion from a very honest paintbrush, that a big fellow, with bishop's crozier and mitre, (*the latter worn hind side before*) was thrusting before her.

A little farther on a female demon was receiving floods of the baptism of life on her forehead, while another, who pretended to be dying, was sent on her long journey with a terrific pouring out of the holy oil.

A master fiend, borne on the shoulders of four others, swung to and fro the most energetic specimen of his satanic and erotic power, and at certain moments he distributed the holy fluid from side to side. Everybody knelt down as he passed. It was called the procession of the holy sacrament.

But suddenly, it strikes one o'clock, and immediately all the demons start calling to one another, join hands and dance round in an enormous circle. The signal is given, they turn round, rise into the air and fly away swift as lightning.

The weaker ones fall down in this mad and giddy flight, this unbridled gallop. Their fall causes others to lose their balance: and there is now but a horrible confusion, a frightful pell-mell of grotesque couplings of hideous love-making, an indescribable chaos of ruined bodies, all soiled with the stains of lust, at last hidden from our sight in a dense cloud of smoke.

GAMIANI: You have a wonderful imagination, Alcide: your dream would look well in a book.

ALCIDE: But listen, I must tell the rest of the story, which is simply the truth, and which really happened. When I came to my senses after this terrible fit, I felt lighter, but weaker. Three women, Still young, and attired in only a white dressing gown, were sitting near my bed.

I thought that my fantastic dream was continuing; but I learnt soon afterwards that my physician, understanding what was the matter with me, had resolved to apply the only remedy suited to my case.

First of all I seized a plump white hand, and covered it with kisses. Fresh and rosy lips came and kissed mine, and this delightful contact electrified me: I felt all the passionate ardour of a wandering maniac.

"Oh, beautiful girls!" I cried, "I want to feel happy, divinely happy: I want to die in your arms. Do submit to my transports, to my madness!"

So saying, I threw off the bedclothes that covered me, and stretched all my length on the bed. A pillow placed under my loins held me in the most advantageous position. My priapus was standing, superb and radiant!

"Thou, o piquant brunette, with the firm white bosom, sit

at the foot of my bed, and stretch thy legs wide apart next to mine. That's right, now take my feet and place

them on thy breasts, rub them gently against thy pretty rosebuds of love. How lovely! Ah, thou art a delightful creature. And thou! 0 blue-eyed blonde, thou shalt be my queen. Come and sit astride on the throne. Take the burning sceptre in one hand, and hide it deep in thy empire. . . Ah, not so quickly. Wait. . . go gently, with up and down movements like a cavalier at a gentle trot. Make the pleasure last. And thou, so tall, so pretty, with thy ravishingly beautiful figure, come and sit down over my head. . . . . ."

"So, that is splendid, thou hast divined what I wanted. Open thy thighs quite wide. . . A little more, so that my eyes may see thee, my mouth devour thee, my tongue penetrate thee at ease. And what art thou doing, standing up so straight? Bend over me, so that I may kiss thy neck."

"Thou art all mine," cried the brunette, showing the tip of her active tongue, pointed and sharp like a Venetian dagger. "Come, let me eat thy eyes, thy mouth. Oh, I love thee so! Oh, naughty lover. . . put thy hand there. . . there. . . go on, gently, slowly. . . . . ."

And we were soon all moving in different ways, all exciting and increasing the pleasure.

This animated scene, these lascivious motions, these extraordinary poses, enchant my eager eyes. Little cries and sighs are heard and mingle very soon: my veins seem to be running with liquid fire. I am trembling all over. My two hands seize a burning hot bosom, or wander madly, grasping still more secret parts. I then began to work with my mouth instead. I sucked eagerly, I nibbled, I bit into the soft flesh! She cried to me to stop, that I was killing her, but I went on more ardently than before.

This overstraining however, finished me. My head fell helplessly to one side, I was exhausted. "Enough, enough," I cried. "Oh, my feet! what a terribly lascivious tickling! You are hurting me. . . You are driving me crazy: my toes stretch out and then clench together. . . Oh!"

I felt the climax approaching for the third time. I pushed away with furious energy. My three beautiful companions all went off into unconsciousness and ecstasy at the same moment and fell together into my arms, beside themselves in the orgasm, and I felt they had drenched me. Were these the joys of heaven or of hell? They were like endless torrents of fire and flame.

GAMIANI: What pleasures you have enjoyed, Alcide. Oh how I envy you! And what about Fanny? I think she has gone to sleep.

FANNY: Leave me now, Gamiani, take your hand away, it is so heavy on me. . . I am overwhelmed. . . dead. . . My God, what a night! Let us sleep. . . I. . . . . .

The poor child yawned, turned round and nestled down in the bed like a tiny baby.

I wanted to bring her back to life, but the Countess said: "No, no, I know just what she must be feeling. Of course I am of a quite different temperament. I feel such irritation within me. . . It torments me, and I am burnt up with desire. Ah, if you only knew how I long for it. I want to have it more and more till it kills me. Your two bodies that I can feel against mine, your talking, our amorous fury, all that excites me, takes me out of myself. Hell is in my mind, fire in my body. I don't know what new device to invent; it is terrible!

ALCIDE: What are you going to do, Gamiani? Are you getting up?

GAMIANI: I cannot lie still, I am on fire. . . I should like. . . but do something to tire me, to wear me out! Squeeze me, beat me. . . Oh, to think that I cannot come!

The Countess' teeth were chattering loudly, her eyes rolled from side to side, she was dreadful to look at, she seemed to be writhing internally, her every muscle was twitching.

Fanny was so shocked and alarmed that she got up. As for me, I was expecting to see her go off into hysterics. In vain I covered her most delicate parts with kisses; my hands were weary of torturing this unconquerable harpie, her secreting canals were closed or emptied. I began to pass blood, but the orgasm, did not occur.

GAMIANI: I shall leave you now, go to sleep!

As she spoke, Gamiani sprang out of bed, opened a door and disappeared from our sight.

ALCIDE: What is it she really wants, do you know, Fanny?

FANNY: Hush, Alcide, listen, what cries! She is killing herself. . . Oh, God, the door is locked! Ah, she has gone into Julie's room. Wait a moment, there is a little window over it, and from thence we shall be able to see everything. Let us bring the sofa over there and two chairs; now get up and let us look.

And what a sight met our eyes! By the changing flicker of a small candle, the Countess, with her eyes rolled up to the whites, foam on her lips, semen all down her thighs, was rolling about and groaning, on a broad rug made of cats' skins.

She was rubbing her back with the greatest agility on the rug. Now and again, the Countess threw her legs up in the air, almost standing thus on her head, showing us all her back; and then fell back with a forced and nervous laugh.

GAMIANI: "Julie, come to me, my head is spinning Ah, you damned fool. I want to bite you."

Julie was naked also, but heavily built and very strong. She seized the Countess' hands and feet and bound them together With cords.

As the excess of passion was driving her mad, her convulsions made me very anxious.

Julie, who seemed absolutely indifferent, was dancing and jumping about like a lunatic, exciting herself at will, and at length having felt the great pleasure of spending, lay back on the armchair. The Countess watched all these movements, and because she could not do the same, could not taste the same delightful intoxication, fell into a renewed rage, twice as terrible as the first. She thought she was a female Prometheus, having her heart torn out by a hundred vultures at once.

GAMIANI: Medor! Medor! Come here, take me!

At the sound of his name, an enormous mastiff rushed out from his kennel, and immediately began to lick her clitoris, the tip of which was standing out between her hairs, red and swollen.

The Countess shouted: Hi, Hi I, still more loudly as the pleasure was becoming more intense. One might thus easily register the degrees of tickling felt by this ungovernable Calymantha.

GAMIANI: Milk, milk! Give me milk!

I was wondering what this cry of agony meant, such a formidable cry of distress; when Julie reappeared, armed with an enormous dildoe filled with hot milk, that had a spring arrangement for spurting the milk ten paces away. With two leather straps, she adapted this ingenious instrument to the right spot on her body. The most bountifully hung stallion, in all his youthful strength, certainly never displayed a more splendid yard, at all events as regards size. I could not imagine it-was possible to introduce this great member, when to my great surprise five or six powerful thrusts, that drew cries of piercing agony from Gamiani, sufficed to push this terrible weapon home to the hilt.

The Countess was suffering hellish torture: she lay stiff and still like the marble statue of Cassandra by Cassini.

Julie was sliding it in and out with great regularity and art, when Medor, mad at being shoved away, came up behind Julie, whose opened backside displayed a most delicious piece of meat, mounted her suddenly, and got it into her so thoroughly that Julie sank down exhausted in a shower of delight.

Such pleasure must indeed be most intense, for it was impossible to imagine a woman enjoying anything so vastly as she did.

Meanwhile the Countess was swearing vigorously at her own pleasure being interrupted, feeling herself tricked out of coming.

But Julie soon came round again, and quickly began with still more vigorous pushing. As the Countess raised her bottom with a jerk to meet one of her strokes, with her eyes closed and mouth open, Julie saw that the critical instant had arrived, so she pressed the spring.

GAMIANI: "Oh, Oh! . . . stop. . . I am melting away. . . hi. . . hi. . . I am spending. . ."

What hellish lubricity! I had not the strength to move from my post of observation. My mind was wandering, my eyes were fascinated.

These furious transports, these brutal fits of lascivity made me giddy. My blood was boiling with voluptuousness, debauchery, and I was raging with lust like a beast.

An extraordinary change had also come over Fanny's expression.

Her eyes were fixed and staring, her arms stiff and nervously clutching me. Her half-parted lips and clenched teeth plainly showed that she too, was longing for this maddening sensuality that approaches frenzy, that is satisfied with nothing but the greatest excesses.

We had scarcely reached our bed again, than we sprang at each other like two wild animals. Our bodies met everywhere, every part of one that rubbed against or pressed the other seemed charged with the strongest electric current. Then in the midst of convulsive embraces, mad cries, passionate sucking and biting all over, we had a frightful coupling of flesh and bone, rapid, excited, all-devouring, but which brought forth only blood from us.

At last we fell asleep from exhaustion, and after five hours of restoring sleep, I was the first to wake.

Brilliant sunshine was streaming in at the windows. The sun's glad rays were piercing the curtains, and playing in golden shimmer, on the rich carpets, the silk hangings.

This enchanting dawn of a new day, coming after a night of riotous debauch, restored me to myself; I thought, how lovely it was to escape from a frightful nightmare. And by my side a sweet creature was lying with a soft white breast, so silky and gentle, so young, so pink and white, that it seemed a sin to touch it even with my lips.

Oh, what a delicious creature was Fanny, as she was lying there, in the arms of Morpheus, half-nude, on a broad oriental divan; she was the idyllic realisation of my most precious dreams.

Her pretty head was lying half resting on one rounded arm, her profile rejoiced my sight, for it was pure and classical like one of Raphael's paintings: her body possessed the purest and most exquisite of outlines.

It was indeed the highest form of voluptuous pleasure to think that these charms were all mine, and it was almost a pity to reflect that after having been virgin for fifteen summers, they had been despoiled in a single night.

Her freshness, her grace, her youth, had all been plunged by the orgy into the filth and the mud of a soulless existence.

This soul of hers, so naïve and tender, this soul that had up to the present been watched over by angels, was to be henceforth the sport of the demons of impurity; no more illusions, no more dreams, no first love, no more sweet surprises: all the poetic dawn of a young girl's life forever ruined. . .

The poor child awoke at last, almost smiling. She thought she was going to find her usual awakening, her innocent thoughts, her purity; but alas! She saw me, and she realised she was no longer in her own room, no longer in her own bed. Oh, her grief hurt me to witness. She melted into tears. I gazed at her, deeply touched. I was frankly ashamed of my conduct. I held her tightly in my arms, and passionately drank every one of her tears.

I no longer felt the overpowering senseless intoxication of the unbridled senses, only my heart went out to her, and she could read my ardent, sincere love in my shining eyes.

Fanny listened, mute, astonished, enchanted; she drank in my words, my very breath, my glances. Every instant she pressed me to her, she seemed to be saying "Yes, yes, I am all thine, all thine." Just as she had given up her body innocent and pure to me, so now she gave her soul, confident, intoxicated with the new sensation of love. I thought to take her soul from her in one wonderful kiss, but it was hers I received in return. It was heavenly and that was the end.

At last we rose.

I desired to see the Countess again. She was a disgusting sight, sprawled out, her body stained and soiled, her face unrecognizable. Like a besotted woman thrown out on the highway, she seemed to be sleeping off her drunkenness of lust.

—"Oh, Fanny, let us go," I cried. . . "let us hurry away from this disgraceful place."

End of the First Part

The skin of the cat as we know, is remarkably exciting, due no doubt, to the large quantity of electricity which it contains. The women of Lesbos invariably used same in their saturnales.

Second Part

I thought that Fanny, being still young, and with an innocent heart, would never remember Gamiani except with feelings of horror and disgust. I surrounded her with affection and loving caresses which were the gentlest and sweetest that I could possibly lavish on anyone. Sometimes I fatigued her with the excess of pleasure, in the hope that she would never again have any liking for other forms of passion than those admitted by nature, which unites the opposite sexes in the pleasures of body and soul.

Alas! I was mistaken.

Her imagination had been perverted, it carried her beyond all our lawful pleasures. In Fanny's eyes nothing could possibly equal the amorous transports of her friend, Gamiani. Our most voluptuous nights seemed to her to be cold, ordinary caresses, compared with the frenzied passion she had known on that fatal night.

She had sworn to me she would never see Gamiani again, but this oath did not extinguish the desire that she nourished secretly. She struggled against it in vain; this inner conflict only resulted in her feeling greatly irritated. I soon realised that she would not be able to resist her desire much longer. I had lost her confidence: and I had to contrive a hiding place in order to watch her.

Having made a spy-hole, cunningly concealed, that gave me a view of her bedroom, I soon saw how unhappy she was. She used to lie on her ottoman and cry, and turn from side to side with a look of desperation on her face. She would then suddenly tear off her clothes and stand naked before her mirror, with a wild look in her eyes.

She used to touch her parts, strike herself, excite herself sensually with an insane and brutal frenzy. I felt that there was no cure for her, but I wanted to see to what ends she would go.

One evening I was at my spy-hole, Fanny was ready for bed, when I heard her cry out:

FANNY: Who's there? Is it you, Angelica? . . . What, it is you, Gamiani! Oh. . . madame, I was far from expecting

GAMIANI: Of course, you avoid me, you drive me away; I have had to resort to stratagem. I have sent your servants away on false pretexts, so now, here I am.

FANNY: I cannot understand you, and still less can I account for your persistence; but if I have kept what I know of you a secret, my flat refusal to receive you ought to have told you plainly enough that your presence here is uncalled for and hateful to me. . . spurn you, I detest you. . . Leave me, I pray of you, avoid creating a scandal.

GAMIANI: My arrangements are made, my mind is made up: you can do nothing against me, Fanny; oh, my patience was quite exhausted.

FANNY: Well, what do you suppose you are going to do now? Do you want to try to take me by force, to outrage me, to drag me in filth. . . Oh no, madame, go away, or I will call my servants.

GAMIANI: My child, we are quite alone; the doors are locked and the keys thrown out of the window. You are mine. . . But don't be alarmed there is nothing to fear.

FANNY: For God's sake, do not touch me.

GAMIANI: Fanny, all resistance is useless. You will always give way to me. I am stronger than you, and I am on fire with passion. No man could overpower me. Ha, ha! she is trembling. . . she has turned quite pale. My God! Fanny, my Fanny. . . She is fainting. Oh, what have I done? Come, wake up, darling. . . wake up. If I hold you thus to my breast, it is for love of you. I love you so dearly, my life, my soul. Why will you not understand me. . . I am not spiteful, my sweetheart, my darling one. . . No, I am good, I am kind to you, for I love you. Look into my eyes, feel how my heart beats. It beats only for you. I only want to see you happy, intoxicated with love in my arms. Oh, let me wake you with my kisses. Oh, what madness. . . I worship, I adore this child.

FANNY: You will kill me. My God I Go away, leave me alone; you are horrible.

GAMIANI: Horrible! . . . horrible? Who then can inspire you with such horror? And am I not a beautiful woman? Am I not still young? Everybody else says so. And my heart: is there one anywhere that can love better than mine? The fire that slumbers within me, that consumes my nature, the burping fire of Italy that doubles my strength and gives me the victory when others are vanquished, is that then a horrible thing? Tell the truth. . . What is a man or a lover compared with me? Two or three rounds of love with a woman and he is done for; if he tries a fourth time, he groans in his failure and his loins give way in the spasm of pleasure. As for me! I remain ever strong, quivering with passion, always fresh, never satisfied. Ah yes, I personify the ardent joys of the thing, the fiery delights of the flesh., Lustful, ever unappeased, I give endless pleasure. I am the love which kills. . .

FANNY: Enough, Gamiani, enough.

GAMIANI: No, no, you shall hear me. Listen Fanny. To lie naked side by side, to feel that we are young and beautiful, soft, perfumed, to be burning with desire and trembling with pleasure; to feel each other, to mingle our beings together, to give up body and spirit in a sigh of satisfied love, only one cry, a cry of love. . . Fanny that is heaven!

FANNY: What a speech! What looks! And I listen to you, I do not drive you away. . . Oh, have pity on me, I am weak and you fascinate me. . . What is then the power you possess? You mix in my flesh and blood, you mingle in my whole being, you are a poison. . . Oh, yes, you are horrible, and yet I love you. . .

GAMIANI: I love you, I love you. Say it again! Oh that is a word that burns.

Gamiani was pale, she knelt motionless, with wide open eyes, with clasped hands before Fanny. She looked as though the heavens had suddenly changed her into marble. She was sublime in her appearance of ecstasy and abnegation.

FANNY: Yes, yes, I love you with all the strength of my nature. I want you, I am dying for you. Oh, I am going mad over you.

GAMIANI: What do you say, my beloved? What is it you say? I am so happy. Your hair is lovely, how silky it is! It slips through my fingers: so golden, and as fine as silk. Your forehead is snowy white and pure, more beautiful than a lily. Your eyes are sweet, your mouth beautiful too. You are white, like satin, with such a natural perfume, an angel from head to foot. You are the angel of voluptuousness. Oh, these dresses, these laces, these strings. . . Take them all off, let me see you naked. . . Be quick, come to me, I am already undressed. Ah, that's fine. You are dazzling. . . Stand up, let me admire your beauty.

If only I could paint, draw your portrait in one moment. . .
Wait, let me kiss your feet, your knees, your breast, your lips.

Kiss me, hold me tight, tighter. Ah, what happiness. . .
what joy. . . She loves me!

The two bodies now made only one. Only the two heads were a little apart, and the eyes looked into each other with a ravishing expression. Their lips were trembling, laughing or glued to each other in ecstasy.

The eyes blazed with passion, the cheeks were quite red. I heard one woman heave a sigh, the other did the same. Then there was a greather, stifled cry, and the two women remained motionless.

FANNY: You made me happy, so happy.
GAMIANI: And I was happy too, Fanny darling, with a happiness
that I had never known before. Our souls and our senses were
united at our lips. . . Let us get on your bed, let us have an
intoxicating night of pleasure!

While speaking thus, they went over to the bed. Fanny lay down first, and stretched herself out voluptuously: Gamiani kneeling at the bedside, drew Fanny to her bosom, and held her in her arms.

Without a word, she looked long at her with devotion. Then they began to sport with each other. They exchanged many kisses, and then their hands got to work, very expert in delicate, exciting touches. Fanny's eyes expressed desire and expectation: Gamiani's showed the disorder of her senses. Flushed in the face and stimulated by the fires of pleasure, they both seemed to my eyes to be simply sparkling all over. These furiously amorous devotees of passion lent poetry to the excess of their lust: they appealed to the senses and the imagination at the same time.

It was no use trying to reason with myself, and to condemn these erotic follies in my heart; I soon felt myself moved, excited, possessed with desire. Finding myself absolutely unable to reach those nude women, I felt like a wild beast tormented at rutting time in a cage, through the bars of which he could see his female.

I stood stupidly still, my head fixed to the aperture whence I was, so to speak, inhaling my torture, a real torture of the damned, terrible, unbearable. A torture that seizes you first by the head, then runs in the blood, then into the bones and the spinal marrow, which seems then to burn. It seemed to me that my nerves were in such a frightful state of tension, that they must break. My clenched bands gripped the floor. I no longer breathed properly, I was foaming at the mouth.

My head turned round and round. I was going mad. I felt my manly force unruly between my fingers, then it stiffened for a moment and dissolved in a shower of burning liquid like a rain of fire. Truly a strange spending, that knocks you over, that leaves you powerless.

As I recovered, I felt enervated. My eyelids were heavy, my head was splitting. I wanted to leave my post: a sigh of Fanny's held me back. The demon of the flesh had conquered me. While my hands grew weary of trying to bring new life back to my manhood, I strained my eyes with trying to see the scene before me, that had so upset my nerves and brain.

The poses of the lovers had changed. My lesbians had crossed each other like two V's, trying to mingle their mossy hairs together, to rub their parts one against the other. They attacked and repelled each others bodies in turn, with a strength and persistence that only the approach of the spasm of pleasure can give to women.

One would have thought, to see them at it, that they were trying to split each other open, to break each others thighs, their efforts were so violent, their breathing so noisy, so gasping.

"Oh dear me," cried Fanny, "I must stop, it is killing me!"

"Go on alone, keep on" . . . answered Gamiani. "I am nearly coming. Push! Go on. . . Now its coming. . . I think I have skinned myself. Ah. . . ah. . . ah."

Fanny's head fell to one side helpless. Gamiani drew her head back, bit into the bedclothes, chewed her hair that floated round her.

I watched their every movement, their transports, and I reached at the same time the height of sensual enjoyment myself.

FANNY: How tired I am! I am worn out, but what lovely pleasure I have had! . . .

GAMIANI: The longer the effort lasts, the harder it is to come, the longer and more intense are our spendings.

FANNY: Yes, I have found that out, I was more than five minutes plunged in a sort of mystic dizziness: I felt the irritation in all my limbs. This rubbing of the hairy mounts of Venus together, with your stiff tuft pressed in my tender lips made the fire of lustful rage stream through my veins. I squirmed and twisted in the luxury of my over-excited genital sense. O madness,

O extremity of joy. . . to spend! Oh, how I understand the meaning of this word now!

One thing however surprises me, Gamiani. How is it that although still young, you know so much about loving sensations? All our extravagances surpass every delight that I thought possible. What is the source of this passion that troubles me, that confounds my judgment, that sometimes frightens me? Nature surely never made us so.

GAMIANI: You would like to know my nature, to hear my history.

Very well Fanny darling, clasp me in your arms, cross your legs round me and I will do the same. I am going to relate my life in the convent. It is a story that may excite us, and that will certainly rouse new desires in us.

FANNY: I am all ears, Gamiani dear.

GAMIANI: You have not forgotten the fearful torture that my aunt inflicted on me, to serve her monstruous lust. The moment I had realised how vile her behaviour to me had been, I collected the necessary documents to guarantee me the use of my fortune. I also took a few jewels and some money, and seizing the opportunity in my aunt's absence, I went for refuge to the Convent of the Nuns of the Redemption.

The Mother Superior, being no doubt touched by my tender age and shy appearance, took me at once to her arms with a loving welcome, so that my fear and anxiety were immediately at an end.

I told her all that had happened, and begged her to shelter me and protect me from my cruel aunt. The superior embraced me affectionately, called me her little girl, and seemed to take me to her heart. Seating me beside her, she related the calm and regular life of the convent: she excited still more the hatred I already felt for men, and concluded with a pious exhortation, that I thought the language of a saint. To render the change from life in the outer world to that of the convent easier for me, she kindly agreed to make me her special protégée, and to allow me to sleep every night in the alcove of her bedroom.

From the second night we were happily chatting of everything like mother and daughter, but the superior could not sleep, she kept turning over in her bed. She complained of the chilly night, and said I should come into her bed, it would be nicer and warmer for both of us. I was surprised to find she was quite naked under the bedclothes.

"One sleeps much better" she said, "without a nightdress." I got into her bed to please her.

"Oh, my little sweetheart," she cried, as she felt my warm body, "you are feverish! How soft and smooth your skin is. What brutes they were to make you suffer so much! Tell me what they really did to you—did they beat you? Tell me everything, sweet child!" So I began to tell her all my story, omitting no detail, even of the most scandalous parts, and these seemed to interest her the most. She felt such intense pleasure listening to me that from time to time she trembled and quivered all over.

"My poor child, my poor little darling!" she kept on repeating, each time pressing me closer into her body.

And then gradually, without exactly realising how it came about, I found myself lying on top of her naked belly and breasts. She had thrown up her legs and crossed them over my loins, her arms were tightly and lovingly clasped round my neck. Her delicious warm odour penetrated me through and through. I began to feel a strange but lovely sensation thrilling my nerves and veins, and that felt as soothing as warm new milk.

As she held me thus pressed to her bosom, I murmured: "Oh, how kind you are to me, so kind that I am happier than I have ever been in my life. I shall never, never want to leave you."

I opened my mouth as I laid my lips over hers, so as to take her loving kisses deeper into my soul, then I began to speak again and said: "Oh, yes! I love you so passionately, I could die for you. . . I don't know what it is, but you make me feel so lovely, it is so nice. . ."

The superior's hands were gently stroking me all over. Her warm body began also to heave and move gently to and fro under me. Her bristling hairy bush between her legs mingled with my tiny silky one, and nearly drove me crazy with its tickling and exciting pricking. I got such thrills all up and down the back that I started to tremble all over. Then as I felt a lingering, deeply penetrating kiss from the superior, I suddenly stopped. "For God's sake, stop. . . let me go. Ah. . ." And my nature came down in such a fragrant shower of dew, too delicious for words.

As soon as this feeling of overwhelming ecstazy had passed a little, instead of feeling at all tired, I threw myself with a newly awakened passion on top of my charming bed-fellow, and smothered her with kisses. Then I took her hand and guided it into the little pinky slit, that she had just been rubbing and exciting so terribly.

The superior could now see for herself how hot I had become, and letting herself go, showed the amorous nature of a Bacchante to the full. We fingered and kissed and tickled and bit each other in a sublime and loving rage. How supple and active were this woman's limbs! Her flexible body bent and writhed in a marvellous manner. I was astounded. I could not keep pace with her. I hardly had time to return one kiss for the thousands that she rained down on every nook and cranny of my passionate young body. I thought she was going to eat me, to devour the parts she loved so well!

This incredible suppleness, this agility in the game of love worked me up to a state of desire and frenzy that I cannot really find words to describe.

Oh, Fanny, what a pity that you were not there to witness our transports of love, our fiery amourous attacks! If you could only have witnessed how erotically mad and breathless we were with our new-found game, you would have fully understood what the overpowering might of sensuality will make of two passionate and loving women!

At one moment I found she had caught my head between her thighs. I thought I could guess what she wanted. Inspired by my own lust, I then began to tongue her in her most secret parts.

But that was not what she desired most. She quickly pulled me up. reversed me over her, and slipping down in the bed, gently, tenderly drew my longing thighs apart, and glued her mouth to me.

Her nervous, quivering, pointed tongue tickled me, pressed me, glided into my roseleaf orifice like a fine dagger, rapidly thrust in and withdrawn from a wound... Her teeth chattered... she seized my clitoris again and seemed to be going to tear my soft flesh... I began to bend about like a snake... I thrust back her head, and, twisted my hands in her long hair.

So then she let go: she touched me more gently still, she forced her spittle into me, licked me slowly, with lingering almost imperceptible tongue, or nibbled and sucked at my maidenhair and my skin with such refined and delicate sensual gentleness that only to think of her loving ways as she did that, makes me spend now. Oh what delights intoxicated me then. What frenzy possessed me! I screamed and groaned with voluptuousness, I fell back exhausted, or stiffened my body in a curve

ALFRED DE MUSSET

like an archer's bow, and still her pointed tongue gave me no respite, still it kept gliding in and out.

Then two thin strong lips took my clitoris, pinched it and sucked it till it drove me mad. No, Fanny, it is quite impossible to feel such sensation and to spend as I spent then more than once in a lifetime.

What extraordinary nervous tension I How my pulses beat! What ardent feelings in all my body, in my blood and brain! I was burning, melting, and I still felt an eager, unsatisfied mouth sucking the essence of my life out of my pussy.

I assure you, Fanny, I was sucked dry when I ought by rights to have been drowned in my own spending and blood. But ah! How supremely happy I was. And, oh Fanny, now I can't wait. . . Whenever I speak of those wonderful times I seem to feel the same devouring sensations. Oh, finish me off. . . Suck more quickly, harder. . . Yes, that's right now, I am coming. . .

Fanny was worse than a starving wolf.

"Enough, enough," Gamiani repeated. "You are draining me dry, you little devil. I did not think you were so clever, so expert, so passionate. But I see you are improving, the fire of lust is going through you."

FANNY: But how can it be otherwise? Any girl must be made of ice, lifeless and without a heart to stay cold with you.—What did you do after that?

GAMIANI: Having learnt so much myself then, I began to exhaust my ardent bedfellow. There was no longer the slightest reserve between us, and I soon learnt that the nuns of the Convent of the Redemption gave themselves fully up to the delights of sensual pleasures, that they had a secret meeting place where they could indulge in safety. Their witches' sabbath used to begin at complines, and terminated with matins.

The superior told me later what was her philosophy, and this shocked me so very much that I thought her the devil incarnate in female form. However, she reassured me by pleasantry and in particular amused me greatly with a description of how she had sacrificed her maidenhead. You could never guess to whom she yielded this treasure; the story is so singular it is really worth while listening to.

The superior, whom I shall call Sainte, was the daughter of a ship-captain. Her mother, a most intelligent woman had

by the devil himself, she hasarded a little hand to grasp it, she touched it, tickled it, caressed it. The ape began to shake all over with raging passion, his grinning was terrible to see. Sainte terrified, thought it was Satan indeed in person. Her terror held her back, but not for long. She was going to run back into the house when one last glance at the tempting long red object decided her to risk it. She pulled her little frock up over her head, and resolutely, bravely, stepped backwards slowly with her bottom offering itself to the dangerous point; the struggle for entrance began, a few sharp strokes, and the ape was doing a man's work for the girl. Sainte was bestialized, raped, violated by the ape. Her joy, her delight were evident by cries of pleasure and pain, but so loud that her mother heard them, and running down the garden path found her little daughter spitted on the virile stake, twisting in agony and throwing her heart up!

FANNY: Oh, what a joke!

GAMIANI: To cure the poor little girl of her bestial love of the monkey, they shut her up in a convent.

FANNY: But it would have better to leave her at the mercy of all the apes!

GAMIANI: You will be able to judge better presently. To return to the story of my stay in the convent: as my temperament was suited to a life of sensuality, I willingly agreed to be initiated into the Dionysian mysteries of monastic life. My application having been accepted by the chapter of the monastery, I was introduced two days later. I arrived naked, as is the rule.

I took the oath required of me, and to conclude the ceremony, prostituted myself with the greatest courage on an enormous wooden priapus specially arranged for this purpose. I had hardly finished a painful and bloody libation when a crowd of the nuns rushed at me, more voracious than a troop of cannibals. I lent myself to all their fancies, I took the most frenetical lubricious poses; finally I executed an obscene dance, and was declared successful. I was exhausted.

A little sister, very lively, very vicious, more subtle than the superior herself, persuaded me to share her bed: she must have been indeed the most cursed tribade that ever came out of Hell. However I fell passionately in love with her wonderful vice, and we were almost always inseparable comrades during the great nocturnal festivals of lust.

FANNY: Where were your Lupercal festivals held?

GAMIANI: In a vast hall which had been decorated and furnished with voluptuous refinement. There were two great portals, hung with Oriental curtains covered with arabesques ànd fringed with gold. On the walls were tapestry plaques of blue velvet in frames of lemon wood, beautifully carved. Lofty mirrors, reaching to the ceiling were set at equal distances on either side. When these orgies were at their height, remarkable groups of delirious nuns participating were reflected in all these mirrors. All round the walls broad divans covered with soft cushions served as resting places, or settings for debauchery. One sank ankle deep in the softest carpets. The curtains, tapestries and even the carpets were woven and worked in a thousand lascivious designs, twenty erotic groups were there shown in every imaginable combination of amorous sport, enough to scourge into activity any desires, no matter how blasé the persons might be. Elsewhere, on the ceiling, in great oil-paintings, the most sensual pictures of debauchery were everywhere displayed. I well remember a certain Thyade with passionate gesture who was being amorously caressed by a Corybante, and it always excited me to the highest degree of sensual pleasure when I looked at it.

FANNY: That must have been delightful to see!

GAMIANI: Then again there were banks of flowers, with the most intoxicating perfume, to charm the eye and complete the decoration. The hall was evenly heated, and six magnificent alabaster lamps diffused a soft agreeable light.

All these arrangements gave birth to new and lovely desires, made one dream of all voluptuous things; it was Oriental, luxurious, poetic. There seemed to be all the mysteries of the harem, all the most secret delights of the East, and an ineffable charm and langourous ease.

FANNY: How lovely it must have been to be able to pass a night there with a beloved companion!

GAMIANI: Yes, surely, Cupid would have made it his own temple, if it had not been transformed every night into a rough and brutal knocking shop.

FANNY: What do you mean?

GAMIANI: As soon as it struck twelve, the nuns filed in, dressed only in a short black tunic that made the whiteness of their skin shine forth in the light of the lamps. Their flowing hair hung round their limbs, their legs were bare. Servants immediately arrived as if by enchantment with every possible luscious food, fruit and drink, which we partook of, reclining on the couches, divans and cushions. Everyone seemed to have a gluttonous appetite and all the good cheer disappeared from sight as if spirited away.

These women were so worn out by their unholy festivals, by the excess of their sexual enjoyments, that by the light of day they were pale and wan, but at night after the feast they began to take on color, and to look less like dead people. The vapors of rich wines, the highly spiced dishes, some seasoned with Spanish fly, set their minds and nerves on fire.

They began to talk loudly, and from obscene words soon came to equally obscene acts, immodest poses, laughter, while songs and cries of the most ribald character, drowned the clinking of wine glasses together, and the popping of corks. The most excited of the nuns, the randiest, fell on her neighbour, and gave her such a sounding kiss that it set the electric spark to the whole neighborhood. The different members of the convent paired off, and enlaced each other in the most vigorous and frenzied embraces. The sound of kisses on the parts of the bodies or the mingling of passionate pairs of lips could be heard, and these finished in sobbing and sighing words of love, or rose to cries of ecstatic abandonment.

It soon happened that the cheeks, the neck breasts and white shoulders failed to satisfy the unbridled desire for kisses. The tunics were pulled up high, or thrown off. Then a wonderful sight met the eye. All these nude bodies of women, supple, gracious, linked naked one to the other, all heaving and moving in unison, pressing each other tightly with the refinement of lust, with the impetuosity of consummate lasciviousness.

If the pleasure was so overwhelming that the final shower was long in coming, a couple would separate to take breath for a moment. The partners gazed into each others shining eyes, burning with desire, and there was a struggle as to which of them should take most attractive posture.

The one who was victorious by her gestures and vicious passion, saw her rival quickly rush to her, throw her over, cover her with kisses, devour her with caresses, devouring literally her most secret dwelling place of pleasure, and placing herself constantly in such a position as to receive the same attacks. The heads of the two nuns were hidden between the thighs of each other, they formed one single body, agitated, excited to convulsions, from which a stifled groan of intense sexual pleasure issued, followed by a triumphal cry of joy!

"They are coming! They're coming!" cried the other damned nuns immediately. And the mad girls threw themselves on one another, more excited and raging than wild beasts in an arena.

In haste to feel the same wonderful sensation of coming in their turn, they tried the most sensational tricks. By dint of leaping around, some of the groups came into collision and fell in a heap on the floor, panting, exhausted with lust and the orgy: a grotesque mélée of naked, freshly excited, half unconscious women heaped up together in the most disgraceful disorder, and this frequently went on until the light of the dawn.

FANNY: What madness!

GAMIANI: They were not satisfied with those things only: they were continually inventing new exercises. Being deprived of the male sex, we were only the more ingenious at inventing extravagant amusements. All the ancient forms of making love and of debauchery, all the obscene stories of ancient and modern times were known to us. We even went beyond them. Elephantis and Aretino had less imagination than we possessed. It would take too long to relate all our tricks, all our subterfuges, our ruses, the marvellous love-philtres that we used to stimulate our wornout nerves, to awaken strange desires and to satisfy them.

It will give you an idea of this if I relate the singular treatment of one our companions in order to excite her passions. First of all she was given a bath of hot blood to renew her vigour. Then she was given a potion to drink, that was prepared with Spanish fly, put to bed, and rubbed all over!

Sometimes she would be hypnotized, and as soon as she was under the influence of the hypnotic sleep, her parts were exposed in an advantageous manner; she was threshed until the blood came, or had needles stuck into her. And the sufferer awoke in the midst of her torture. She looked quite wandering in her mind and immediately went into violent convulsions.

It took six persons to hold her down, and nothing appeared to calm her but the licking of a dog. And then if her madness continued and the sexual orgasm did not occur, the unhappy woman became still more furious and shouted in a loud voice that she wanted an ass.

FANNY: What, an ass? Good Gracious!

GAMIANI: Yes, my dear, an ass. We had two that were thoroughly trained and tame. We did not wish to lag behind those ladies of ancient Rome who used them regularly in their saturnalia.

The first time that one was tried on me, I was quite drunk with wine: I threw myself violently on the little seat specially placed, braving all the nuns. The ass was brought into position in front of me at once with the help of an arrangement of leather straps. His terrible weapon, warmed up by the sisters' hands, struck heavily on my side. I seized it in both hands, placed it at my orifice, and after tickling myself with it for a few seconds, I tried to get it in. I stretched myself with my fingers, the nuns had greased me with an expanding salve, and rising to meet him, I gradually managed to get at least five inches inside of me.

I wanted to push again, to get still more in, but my strength was not equal to it, and I fell back. It seemed to me that all my flesh was being ripped open, that I was split in two, dismembered I It was a dull, stifling pain, to which however there came a vicient irritation, exciting, tickling, sensual. The animal by dint of continual moving, caused such a vigorous friction that all my bones seemed to be disjointed. The canals and glands of my secretions opened and flooded me, and my burning opening trembled and shook for an instant right to the middle of my back. Oh what an extraordinary spending! What an orgasm! I felt it shoot from me like spurts of flame, and then fall drop by drop to the bottom of my womb. Everything in my inmost being was steaming with lust. I uttered one long cry of nervous ecstasy and was relieved.

In my frantic lustful plunging I had actually got two more inches of the weapon in me, and if it had not been stopped by the animals fleshy sheath, he would have disembowelled me. I had beaten every record, my comrades were beaten hollow.

Exhausted, throbbing with pain in every limb, I thought my voluptuous enjoyment over, when the plaguey thing stiffened and swelled in me still stronger than before, thrust right in me still deeper, almost lifted me bodily on its stiff standing shaft. I gnashed my teeth, clenched my fists, my hands held my poor thighs tightly. Then suddenly a stream of thick pungent hot seed was shot into my womb, so violently that it seemed to flood my heart and overflow my arteries and veins.

My body was then calmed and relaxed in its every part, instead of agonizing pain, I felt only delicious but excruciating sensations, as though this frightful balsamic injection had brought me such a climax of supernatural ecstasy that nerves and brain melted into one heavenly annihilation. . . Delicious torture. . . Sweet pain. . . That loosens the bonds of life and kills with intoxicating joy! . . .

FANNY: What feelings you make run through me, Gamiani! I cannot keep my feelings and desires back much longer. . . But really how did you finally escape from this devilish convent?

GAMIANI: Well, I will tell you: after one of our great orgies, we had the idea of turning ourselves into men by wearing dildoes, and to connect our comrades before and behind us in a chain, then to run round in a ring like mad things, each nun having a dildoe up her from behind, and rendering a like service to the nun in front of her with the dildoe she was wearing herself. On this occasion I was the last one in the chain so that there was no dildoe to satisfy me behind. What was my surprise as I felt I was being ravished by an unknown man from behind. How he had got into our party I did not know. At the shriek I uttered, the chain of nuns dissolved, and they all came rushing on him.

Every one of the girls was tired of artificial instruments, and insisted on him giving her the real thing. The too happy man was soon worn out and done for. You should have seen

ALFRED DE MUSSET

his weapon hanging thin and useless, his expression of utter fatigue, all his manhood nonexistent. I had the greatest difficulty in arousing this human rag when my turn came to taste his elixir. However, I managed it. I lay on the dying man, with my head between his thighs and sucked off his priapus so cleverly that it raised its rosy head once more. Some girl behind me was tongueing my orifice at the same time so that I soon felt I was coming fast. Quickly turning round I impaled myself on the standing sceptre that I had awakened so successfully, and was rewarded by a shower that I returned instantly with my own spending.

This final success finished our poor man off. We tried everything possible to call him back to life, all was useless. Well, would you believe it? As soon as these nuns found out that he was no more good that night, they resolved to kill him outright and bury him in one of their cellars for fear he would split on them outside and cause a scandal concerning the convent.

I begged them not to do this, but in a second they had let down one of the hanging lamps, and attached the cord round his neck, then as they pulled him up, and hanged him, I turned my eyes away from the horrible sight. But to the great surprise of the mad creatures, the hanging produced a not unusual effect. Surprised and delighted at this nervous and muscular demonstration the superior took a ladder, and mounting to the proper height impaled herself on the projection, and thus married a corpse in mid-air to the frenzied applause of her worthy accomplices.

This however, is not quite the end of the story. The rope was too thin or worn to support the weight of two bodies, so it broke, and the dying man and living woman fell to the ground together so heavily that she broke both her legs, and the cord loosening, the dying man came to life sufficiently to try to strangle the superior with a death grip in his expiring convulsions.

The fall of a thunderbolt would not have caused more consternation amongst the nuns than this event. They all scattered, frightened to death that Satan himself was amongst them. The superior was lying alone trying to fight off the desperate dying man.

The adventure might have had most serious consequences, so, in order to get away from it all, I escaped that night from this den of crime and debauchery.

I stayed some little time at Florence, the abode of love and distinction. A young English nobleman, Sir Edward X..., poetic and a dreamer like Oswald, fell violently in love with me. I was sick of disgusting amusements. Up to that time my physical senses alone had been awakened, my soul still slumbered. It was gently awakened by the pure and sweet accents of a disinterested and noble love. I began to understand the beauties of a new existence: I felt vague and inexpressible desires that lent poetry and happiness to my life...

Combustible substances do not catch fire of themselves; but a spark is often enough to set them burning! In this manner my heart was inflamed by the passionate declarations of my lover. When I heard the accents of this new language, I felt a sweet trembling go right through me, I listened attentively; my eager eyes lost no expression of his beloved features. The flame that came forth from my lover's eyes penetrated to the depths of my soul and agitated me, making me transcendently happy at the same time. Edward's voice thrilled me with its vibrations. Every gesture of his seemed to me pregnant with sentiment; the passion written on his face and in his eyes found an echo in my own. I was as eager and intense in living for the heart as I had been in living for the senses alone. Edward had one of those lofty, powerful minds that lifts others up to his level. Love became exalted, sublimated in me,—the mere thought of sensual pleasures revolted me. If I had been violated, I felt that I should die of rage. This voluntary barrier torturing the passions of us both, our love only became more ardent in consequence.

Edward was the first to give way. Tired of a Platonic affection of which he ignored the cause, he was no longer possessed of sufficient force of character to control his passions. Finding me one day fast asleep he took me for himself... I awoke in the midst of the most ardent embraces; lost to the world, I replied to his transports of joy with my own; I was three times in the clouds, Edward was three times god-like, but as he fell back from me and lay at my side, I felt only horror of him—for me he was now nothing more than a man of flesh and blood, like the monk who had taken my maidenhead!

I escaped immediately, with fearfully sardonic laughter. The idol was broken; a wind of impurity had extinguished the spark of love; this divine spark that only burns once in one's life; my soul no longer existed. The senses came to the surface, and I returned to my former life. . .

FANNY: You returned to the love of women?

GAMIANI: No! First of all I wanted to break with men. In order to kill all trace of desire for them or of regret, I ran the round of all the pleasures men can give us. I placed myself in the hands of a celebrated procuress. She found men for me and they were the most expert and muscular Hercules of the city of Florence. It has really happened that I have run as many as thirty two courses in one morning, and still want more. Six athletes were knocked out by me. But one evening I did better than that. I was with three of my most powerful champions. My behaviour and my words put them in such good humour that a devilish idea came to me. To try it out, I begged the strongest one to lie on his back, and while I was enjoying myself to the full on his machine, which was a monster, I was quickly sodomised by the second; my mouth got to work on the third one, and caused him such excitement that he writhed about like a demon, and uttered the most passionate cries. All at once the four of us got the wonderful orgasmal sensation and came down in a perfect shower at the self-same instant. What ardent enjoyment of taste to my palate I What delicious intoxicating overflow in my entrails I Can you conceive these excesses? Just fancy I To suck in one's mouth all a man's love-juice and strength; and impatiently to drink it, to swallow it in waves of foam both warm and bitter, and at the same time to feel a double jet of flame enter your body by its two lower orifices at once. It is a triple pleasure, impossible to adequately describe. My incomparable strong men were polite enough to do it over and over again as long as their strength permitted.

Since that time, fatigued, disgusted with men, I have never been able to understand or experience real pleasure, except when I could hold in my loving arms the slender naked trembling body of an innocent young girl, still virgin, whom one can initiate and teach the arts of love, who is surprised, astonished and then charmed at the unknown sensations. . . But. . . what is the matter with you? What are you doing?

FANNY: Oh, I am in a terrible state. I feel horrible, monstruous desires invading my being. Now after hearing all this, I feel I, too, want to know all these sensations, to go through all you have gone through. Whether it brings me pleasure or pain, I want to lie in your dear arms, but not bye and bye, now immediately. . . But you alone cannot satisfy me perhaps. . . My poor head is throbbing. . . Turning round giddily. . . Oh, I am afraid I shall go mad.

Come, show me what you can do for me. I want to die in your arms from excess of sensuality. I want to spend, to come, at last to spend in an endless shower!

GAMIANI: Calm yourself Fanny! Calm down! Your eyes look so wild, you really frighten me. I will do anything you like, what do you order me to do for you?

FANNY: Well, I want your dear mouth to take me, suck me off. . . There, there, make me die of pleasure. After that, I want to take you too, to plunge into your entrails and to make you scream! . . . Oh, when I think of that ass! It torments my mind. I want an enormous member thrust in me, even if it should split me open and make me die like a bitch.

GAMIANI: You are perfectly mad, you will be satisfied. My mouth and tongue are expert, and besides I have brought a nice instrument. Look. . . it is as good as the action of an ass!

FANNY: Ah. . . what a monster! Let me try it at once. Oh. . . ah. . . it is too big, impossible. . . It stifles me!

GAMIANI: You don't know how to point it. That's my business. Only don't be afraid, hold tight and be brave.

FANNY: Even if it should cost me my life, I want to take it all in; I am on fire!

GAMIANI: Lie on your back with your limbs loosely relaxed, let your arms hang down and spread your thighs as widely opened as possible, and let your beautiful long hair stream out around your head. Let me take you without fear and without reserve.

FANNY: O yes, I will give myself wholly up to you with delight. Come to my arms, come quickly!

GAMIANI: Patience, child. Listen, in order to feel all, all the pleasure that I can give you, you must forget yourself for an instant, lose yourself, melt into one thought only, the thought of sensual love, of fleshly rapture and mad delight. No matter what way I may attack you, no matter with what rage and force, you must not budge or give an answering movement. Lie quite still and receive my caresses and kisses without returning them. If I bite you, if I tear your flesh, stifle all cries of pain as well as of pleasure until the moment comes when we will both work and struggle together so as to die of pleasure at the same time in each others arms.

FANNY: Oh, yes, I quite understand, Gamiani. Let us begin, I am like a sleeping girl, now I am dreaming. I am waiting for you, come. Am I placed right now? Wait a bit, I think this pose will be still more lascivious.

GAMIANI: Little vicious one! You surpass me. How lovely you are, showing everything like that. . . How impatient you are I You want it all already, I can see that. . .

FANNY: Say rather I am on fire with lust. Begin, oh do begin!

GAMIANI: Oh, let us keep up this delightful preparation a little longer. It is so delightful. Relax a little more. Ah, so is very well. You look as though you were dead. . . delicious abandonment. That's right. Now I am going to seize you, warm you up, bring you gradually back to life. I am going to set your feelings on fire, to raise you to the heights of sensual delight. Then you will fall again as if dead, but dying of pleasure and of excesses. Delightful unknown things! To taste these joys for two seconds only will be a god-like joy!

FANNY: Your speech tortures me with inward fire. Get on with it, Gamiani.

At these words, Gamiani hastily did her hair that was flying round her, up into a knot. She pressed her hand for a moment on her sex, to excite it and then sprang on Fanny's body, which she touched, and then covered all over. Her lips opened the rose-like mouth of Fanny, her tongue then drew out the honey. Fanny exhaled a sigh; Gamiani drank it in and stopped. To see these two women naked, motionless, and locked one in the others arms, one might have imagined that a subtle and mysterious fusion of their souls and bodies had taken place in silence.

Insensibly Gamiani lossened her embrace and rose. Her fingers were then playing capriciously with Fanny's hair which she gazed at with an enchanted smile of languor and voluptuousness. Kisses and soft nibbling bites now flew all over Fanny from head to foot, and Gamiani's tongue tickled her between the toes.

She then rises again erect, and returned to the attack, and falls back on her again, panting, and voracious. Her head and hands caress her all over at once. Fanny is kissed, rubbed, manipulated in her every part, she is pinched, squeezed and bitten. Her courage gives way, she begins to scream; but a delightful fingering brings her back to reason and she stops whimpering and brings forth a long-drawn sigh. Still more ardent, still more furiously lustful, Gamiani throws her head down between Fanny's thighs. Her fingers tear Fanny's roseleaf lips violently asunder. Her long pointed tongue plunges in the depths, and slowly she exhausts all the delights of "minette," the most irritant tickling that any woman can possibly experience.

Carefully noting the degree of delirium she is provoking, she stops or redoubles her attentions, according as the excess of pleasure hastens or retards the climax.

Fanny, her nerves in a frightful state, all at once goes into a convulsion.

FANNY: Oh, that's too much, I can't bear it. . . oh dear!

GAMIANI: Take it, drink it then, said the Countess, handing her a phial of which she had just drunk half the contents. Drink! It is the elixir of life. It will renew your strength.

Fanny, exhausted, powerless to resist, drinks the liqueur that was poured into her half-open mouth.

"Ha, ha!" cries Gamiani in a triumphant voice, "now you are mine!" Her glance had something infernal in it.

Kneeling between Fanny's legs, she strapped on her terrible instrument and brandished it with a menacing air.

ALFRED DE MUSSET

When she saw it, Fanny's convulsive movements redoubled in intensity. An internal fire seemed about to consume her and stimulated her to frenzy. Her widespread thighs prepared with an effort to receive the monstruous model of a priapus.

The mad thing! She had hardly accepted the terrible martyrdom when a strange convulsive movement made her start from side to side.

> FANNY: Ah, my God, oh, dear me! That liqueur is burning my entrails. Ah how it pains me, how it burns me. . . Oh, I am going to die! Vile damned witch, you have got me. . . you have got me now. . . ah!

Gamiani, heedless of her cries of anguish and of torture, redoubled her attack. She tears through everything, and swims in a bath of blood; but now it is her own turn. Her limbs twist in cramp, the bones, and joints of her fingers crack. I have no longer any doubt that she has swallowed and given a violent poison. Horrified, I rush to their help. I force open the doors in my anger. Alas! Fanny had ceased to breathe. Her arms and legs, clasped in the convulsions of a horrible death are entwined in Gamiani's who was just breathing and gasping in her struggle against death.

I tried to part them.

"Don't you see," a dying voice said, "that the poison is killing me. . . that my sinews are twisting. Go away. . . This woman is mine! Ha, ha!"

"Ah, it's terrible!" I cried, beside myself.

> GAMIANI: Ah, yes. But I have known all the excesses of sensuality in the torture caused by the poison. If, in the martyrdom of another woman mingled with my own, there was any possible sensuality. It is atrocious! Do you hear! I am dying in the rage of passion, mad, quite mad! Don't you understand. I only wanted to know, if I could not do more in the rage of agony! Alas, alas!

At this long cry, that came from a hollowed breast, the horrible fury of a woman fell dead on the corpse of her victim!

FINIS

A Note About the Author

Alfred de Musset (1810–1857) was a French poet, novelist, and dramatist. Born in Paris, he was raised in an upper-class family. Gifted from a young age, he showed an early interest in acting and storytelling and excelled as a student at the Lycée Henri-IV. After trying his hand at careers in law, art, and medicine, de Musset published his debut collection of poems to widespread acclaim. Recognized as a pioneering Romanticist, de Musset would base his most famous work, *The Confession of a Child of the Century* (1836), on his two-year love affair with French novelist George Sand. Although published anonymously, de Musset has also been identified as the author of *Gamiani, or Two Passionate Nights* (1833), a lesbian erotic novel. Believed to have been inspired by Sand, who dressed in men's attire and pursued relationships with men and women throughout her life, *Gamiani, or Two Passionate Nights* was an immediate bestseller in France.

A Note from the Publisher

Spanning many genres, from non-fiction essays to literature classics to children's books and lyric poetry, Mint Edition books showcase the master works of our time in a modern new package. The text is freshly typeset, is clean and easy to read, and features a new note about the author in each volume. Many books also include exclusive new introductory material. Every book boasts a striking new cover, which makes it as appropriate for collecting as it is for gift giving. Mint Edition books are only printed when a reader orders them, so natural resources are not wasted. We're proud that our books are never manufactured in excess and exist only in the exact quantity they need to be read and enjoyed.

Discover more of your favorite classics with Bookfinity™.

- Track your reading with custom book lists.
- Get great book recommendations for your personalized Reader Type.
- Add reviews for your favorite books.
- AND MUCH MORE!

Visit **bookfinity.com** and take the fun Reader Type quiz to get started.

Enjoy our classic and modern companion pairings!